Sprout
The
Mighty Oak

By

Donna Watkins and Caden Beavers

Disclaimer

Story Text written by Donna Watkins

Interior Artwork provided by Caden Beavers

Book Cover provided by Carol Dabney

Copyright

From Seed to Tree – the amazing story of an Oak Tree growing in a forest with her tree family who nurtures, shares, and protects her until she grows into a massive tree. Trees, animals, and people all need each other to survive. This inter-dependence is beautifully displayed as Sprout The Mighty Oak shares her story inside the pages of this book.

Are you looking way up in the sky trying to see where my largest branches end and the clouds begin? I'm a massive mighty oak tree rooted in the ground at the edge of a forest.

Several years ago, a forester gave me the name Sprout. It is hard to believe that was

150 years ago when my tiny crown of leaves first broke through the ground.

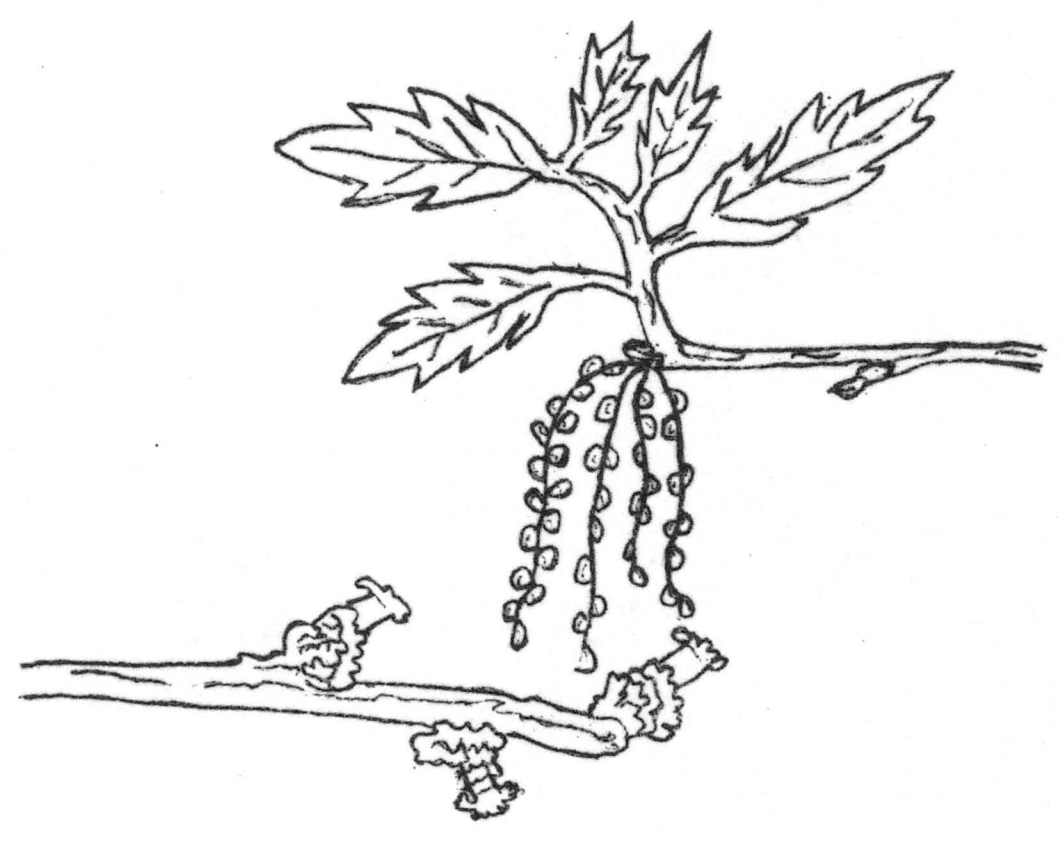

In the beginning of my life as a new tree the wind pollinated an oak flower on a mature oak tree which developed into an acorn on a twig.

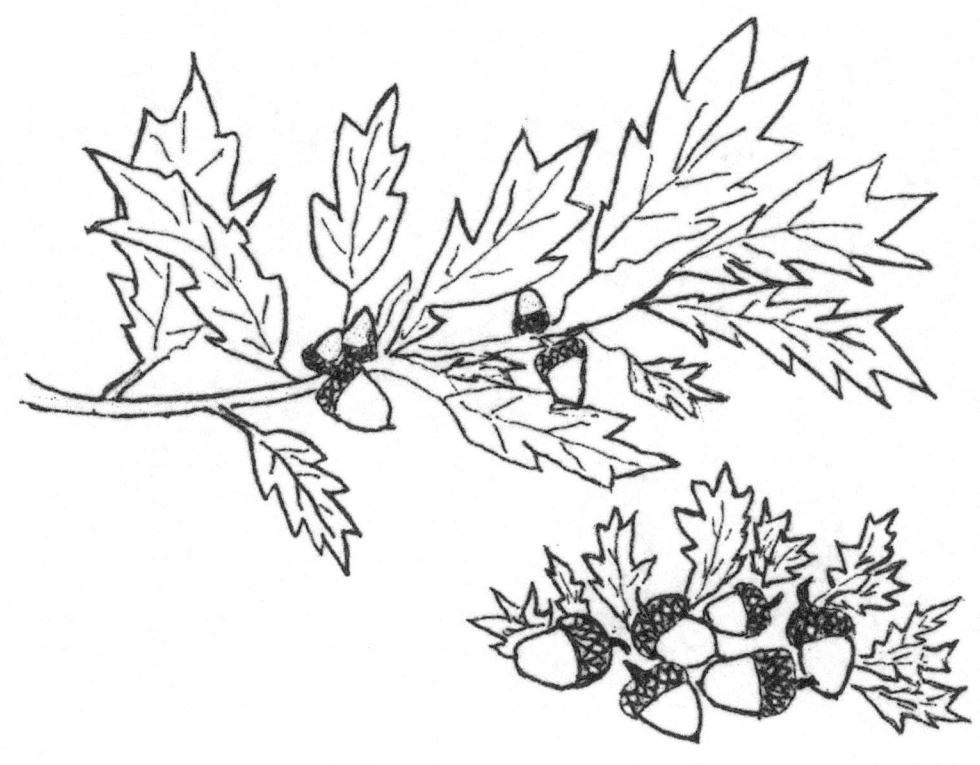

As an acorn, I began to grow and change. After I ripened on the twig for several

months, I dropped to the ground to huddle among a layered clutter of leaves and

loose soil.

As the ground was softened by rain, I worked my way down into the dirt where I developed a root which fastened me securely into my spot. During the winter my root continued to grow.

When the warmth of spring arrived, my shell cracked open and I sprouted into new growth from my pointed root end. My stem was working its way up through the soil in search of sunshine.

As I surfaced the ground, my slender plant body stretched upward and my tender small leaves unfolded as a tiny infant tree called a seedling or 'Sprout'. Nutrients stored inside my acorn shell by my Mother Tree provided food for me to grow for months. Later, as I developed enough leaves, I gathered food and water from the soil and sunlight.

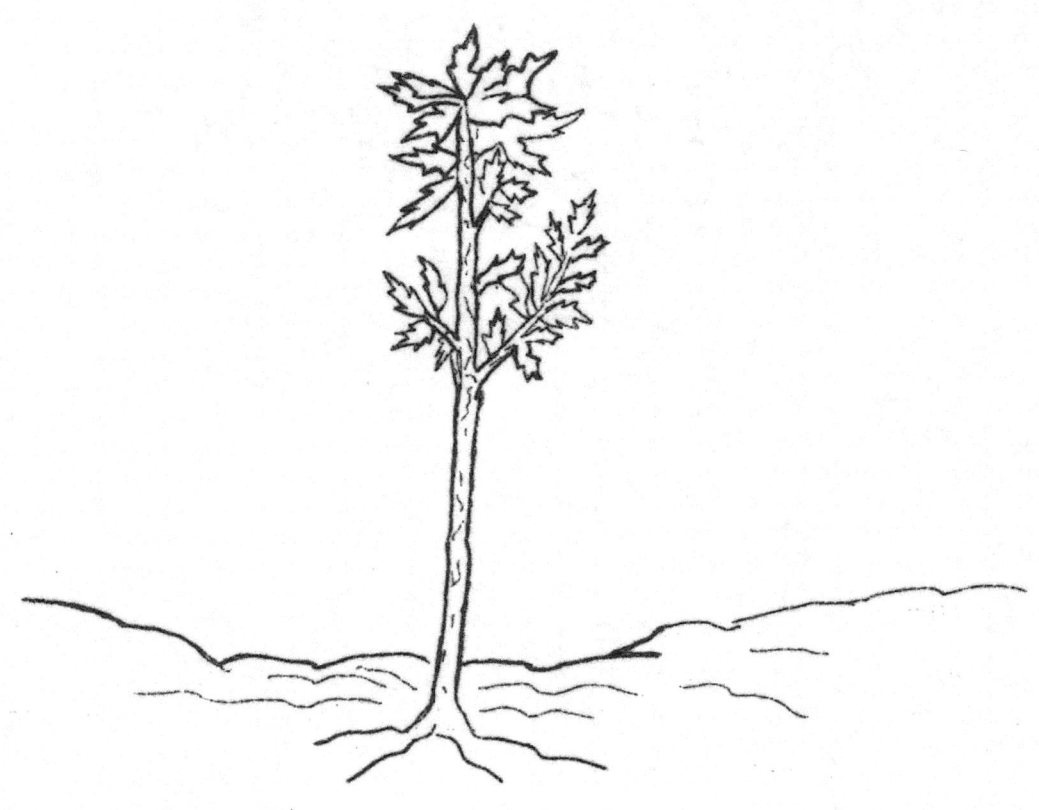

After growing for a few years, I became a taller more sturdy youth known as a

Sapling.

At about thirteen years of age, I reached the gangly thin teenager part of my life where I was known as a Pole tree. This is the stage of life that I grew more quickly and was well on my way to growing into a tall strong massive oak tree.

I couldn't wait to grow up and produce acorns myself. The other trees in the forest

informed it would take patience for me to reach the maturity to grow my own

acorns. The process would take between 20 to 50 years. That seemed like a very long

time!

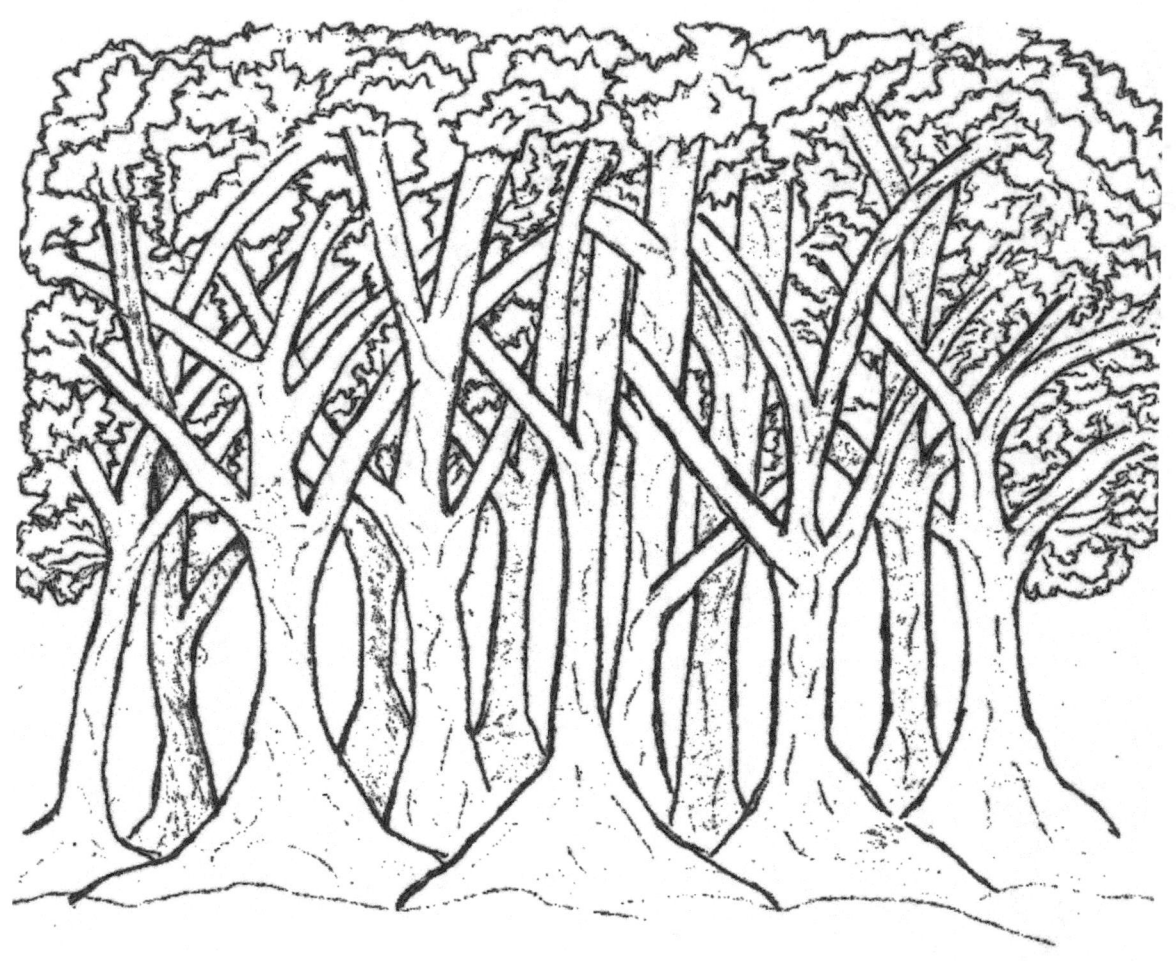

Just like you, when I was young I always liked secrets, surprises, and mysteries. It made me feel special when an Old Mother Tree shared the secret of tree survival. "Sprout, " she said, "Just like all living things, trees have families. Trees need each other to survive. We take care of each other."

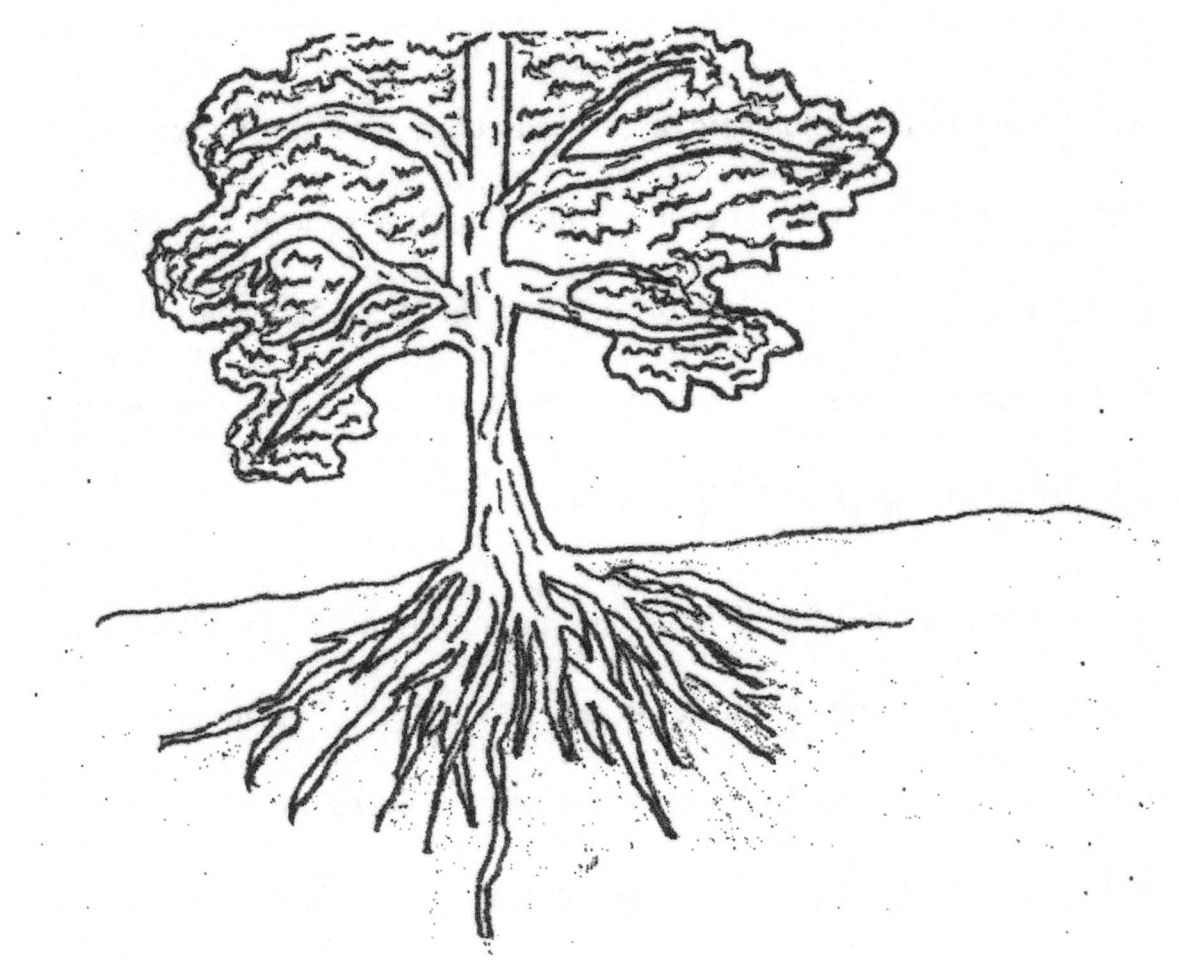

The Old Oak revealed that if I grew weak or got sick during my time of growth, other trees would share nutrients and water with me through our connected roots beneath the ground. From young sprouts to old tree stumps, the Colony of trees would sacrifice some of their food and water to send their way.

She also advised that trees communicate messages to each other through chemical codes, electrical impulses, and fungal nettings around our tree root tips. Trees also communicate through sense of smell and taste. This is the tree language used to inform each other about sickness and dangers. When a tree needs help, it sends out a message and the other trees provide aid.

It is a secret connection going on deep in the dirt where tree roots and fungus send messages and above the ground where leaves release scents into the air. Trees even use the sense of touch. Trees growing next to each other grow upward instead of outward into the growing space of neighboring trees. Although plants, animals, and human beings have different methods of communicating, all of them depend upon each other for their survival.

From tree top canopies sheltering smaller trees in the understory from the weather
to food being shared through connected roots, to signals being sent about the
dangers of insects and animals, Tree Families protect each other. As a young tree,
receiving this information made me feel safe and secure.

Mother Oak also informed me that oak trees are so special that we have been designated as the National Tree of America as well as several other countries. That news made me feel proud! I was then determined to be the biggest strongest oak that I could be. Someday, I might grow to be 90 feet tall!

As a fully grown tree, I could be valuable for many reasons. As a standing tree, my strong root system can prevent flooding and soil erosion. My leaves can help clean the air, generate oxygen, cool the atmosphere, create shade for people, and provide safe shelter for birds and other creatures. My limbs can break the speed of winds and muffle sounds. My acorn nuts can provide food for wildlife. My trunk can provide valuable timber for building.

As we all know, time passes fast. Surprisingly, on my 30th birthday, I grew about 2000 acorns. I was quite proud of the number, although as I aged there would be a much larger crop. During the fall season, my acorns drop to the ground and provide food for many animals such as deer, squirrels, mice, rabbits, raccoons, opossums, foxes, bears and other animals. Several species of fowl and birds can feed on my acorns as well; these include wild turkey, quail, ducks, woodpeckers and blue jays.

Leaves, stems, and twigs on my branches may provide a stable food source for animals during times of food shortages. Even the leaf debris and decaying nuts on the ground are beneficial as they provide food for insects, frogs, lizards, and fungi.

When I reached the age of 50 years old, I produced a mast of acorns which would number around 10,000 nuts in all. Usually, there are so many acorns the animals can have their food and some acorns are left to grow into more new trees. Oak trees are part of the earth's system where species help each other. Mother Nature tries to keep this balance of interdependence in order. Plants, animals, birds, reptiles, and insects all need each other in order to exist. Human beings play a role in this system as well.

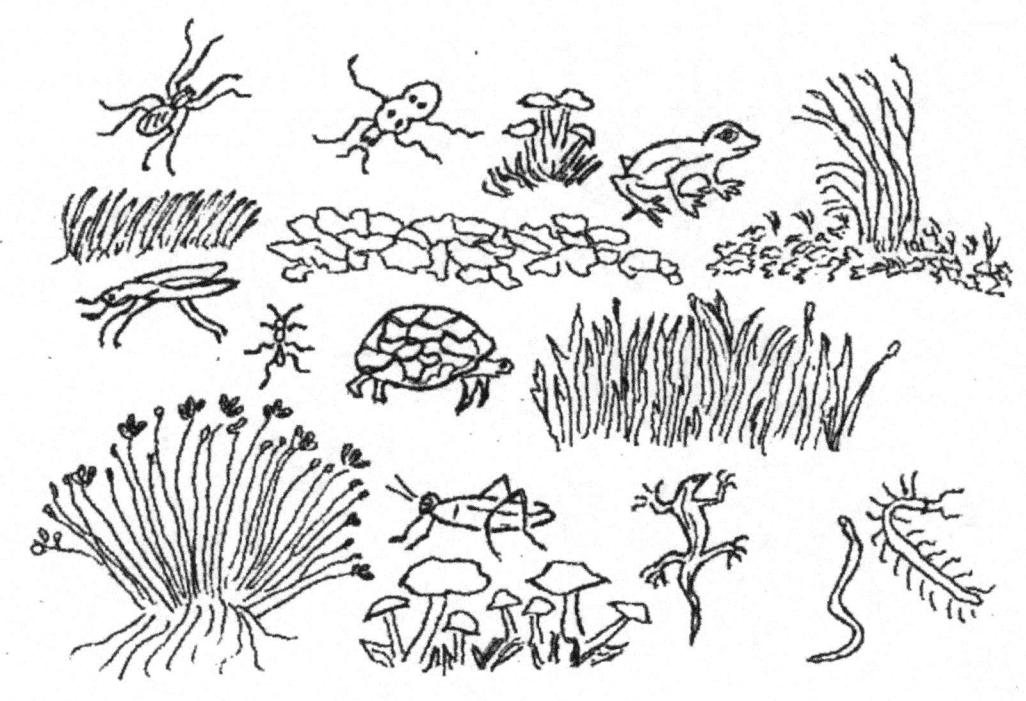

My life cycle continues. As the winter months approach, my leaves turn color then I shed them and they fall to the ground. After my oak leaves have fallen and dried out, I continue to provide shelter to many small creatures like worms, ants, slugs, beetles, lizards and spiders which live in the layers of dead leaves that accumulate on top of the soil.

Even holes in my trunk are used as roost nests by some animals and birds. It seems

every part of me is useful.

As a gift from nature, one of my strong branches could make a great place to hang a

child's swing or support a tree house!

The average lifespan for an oak tree is between 200 – 600 years, although some special species of oaks can live thousands of years. I might live that long or I might be more useful providing products to benefit others. I am a white oak which makes me especially strong and sturdy.

Timber from oaks like me has been used for generations of time to build everything from tiny log houses to massive castles and small fishing boats to Viking ships. It has been said that Christopher Columbus' trip across the ocean to discover America was made in a vessel made of oak and pine. I think that particular species of oak was 'cork oak' which is my cousin. Cork wood helps buoy up a ship.

You might be curious about how trees like me are cut and used for commercial purposes. People grow plant crops for food and they also grow trees as crops. Unlike food crops which are seasonal, tree crops take many years to grow. Timber may be harvested from trees grown on huge tree farms where hundreds of trees are growing about the same age and species. Some timber is harvested from stands of trees in forests where trees of a variety of species and ages grow together.

When trees reach maturity on a tree farm, the entire section of mature trees is cut

down. In a forest setting, specific trees are tagged to be cut and removed. The trees

are then hauled to the lumber yard to be processed. At the lumber yard, the trees

are stripped of their bark and small branches, then, seasoned to remove the water in

the wood. Preservatives may be added to the wood as a treatment to make it last

longer.

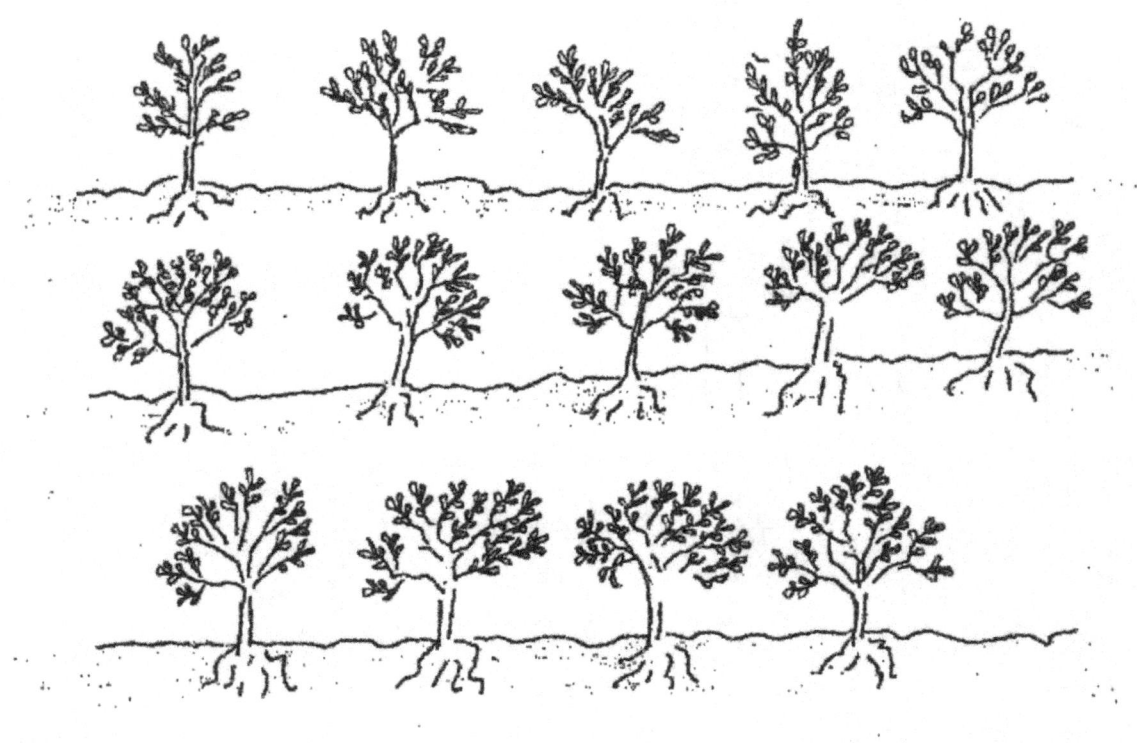

Forests are a very important part of our world. Our forests can be strengthened and preserved by select cutting of trees instead of mass cutting. Saving some of the mother trees from being cut allows nourishment to younger growing trees which keeps the forest healthy. It is also very important to plant many new trees. Replacing cut trees with newly planted trees is practicing good earth stewardship.

Trees have been a part of our planet's eco-system which has balanced and nurtured life throughout our existence. Standing trees help the environment. Cut trees provide timber for building things and pulp for making wood products. Countless things man uses are made from wood. I could stand in the ground until I am 600 years old and be a part of nature, or, if I am selected to be cut for commercial use, I can be used for so many practical things. Just look at the partial list of wood uses on the next page and you will be impressed.

Buildings –bowls – books – bulletin boards – banjos – bookshelves – beds – baseball bats – benches – bird houses – bat houses – bath houses – broom handles – broom straws – barrels – boxes – bagpipes – chairs – cabinets – crates – cages - cardboard boxes – candy wrappers – chop sticks –cereal boxes – cutting boards – combs – canes –copy paper – doors – decks - dog houses – duck decoys – drummer sticks – diapers – egg cartons – furniture – flooring – fence posts – fire wood – fishing corks – guitars - grocery bags – gift wrap - golf tees – greeting cards – houses – hand rails - kites – kleenex - labels – ladders - matches - magazines – mailing envelopes – milk cartons – measuring sticks - notebook paper – napkins - newspapers – piano keys - price tags – posters - paper – paper towels – paper plates – paper cups – postage stamps - picture frames – pool sticks –ping pong paddles – pencils – pointers – pallets – porches –railroad ties –stair steps –stools – shelves – shingles - tool handles - toilet paper – tables – tongue depressors – tooth picks - window frames - window blinds – wooden spoons – wood beams – wooden blocks – and much much more! It would be fun to try to name more things made from wood like me. Try it!

In the meantime, help keep the earth healthy by planting more trees. And, you can start by simply planting an acorn in the ground to grow into a mighty oak tree – just like me! Find the perfect spot and plant your acorn. Place a marker at the site so that you don't forget where you planted. Be sure the plant site has water and keep it clear of weeds. Plant your acorn in the Fall and watch a brand new sprout shoot up out of the dirt the next Spring!

Step by Step Instructions to Plant Your Acorn: During the months of September through November acorns begin to ripen and drop to the ground. When acorns are fully ripened, you may pick them from the tree or collect them from the ground after they have fallen.

It would be very hard to collect acorns from the ground in a forest setting so try to locate an oak tree in your neighborhood or community such as municipal areas, churches, or schools. Always remember to ask permission to pick acorns on other people's property.

If possible, pick acorns directly from trees. When you shake the branch and the acorn separates easily from its cap, it is ready for picking. The cap is a separate protective covering and not a part of the actual acorn itself.

If you pick acorns up from the ground, sort through them carefully to make sure they are not damaged from insect bored holes or soil rot. Acorns which have dried out will not germinate.

To check the health of the acorns, place them (capless) into a bucket of water. Give them a couple of minutes to sort. The defective acorns will float to the top of the water - discard these acorns. Drain and dry the good ones.

It is best to plant your acorns immediately. If that is not possible, acorns can be stored in the refrigerator in a tightly sealed heavy freezer bag along with some damp peat soil mix. Do not freeze acorns as this will destroy them.

When it is Spring-time, dig a 2 inch deep hole in the ground and plant 2 to 4 acorns on their sides about 6 inches apart. Cover the acorns with loose dirt; pat down; then cover with a couple inches of good mulch. Mulch conserves moisture in the soil and helps retard weed growth which competes with the emerging oak sprout which should pop out of the ground about three months after planting.

Water the planting site frequently to keep it moist and watch for your tree 'Sprout' to pop out of the ground. You might want to place an empty gallon milk jug that has the bottom and top cut out of it over the planting area to keep critters from digging up your acorn or munching on the new sprout.

It is very important to choose the proper location for your newly developing oak tree. Because oak trees can grow to be very large trees, there must be plenty of space for the tree to stand after it matures which takes years. Don't plant too close the house, driveway, power lines, or septic lines or tanks.

If there is no space available for a large shade tree, you might want to plant a much smaller ornamental tree in your yard and many of these ornamentals bear beautiful showy flower buds.

So be it big or small, just go out and plant a tree for a healthy environment. Be sure to give 'your tree' a name because the two of you will be friends for a lifetime!

Author Biographies:

Donna Watkins is an Arkansas word scriber who pens words to books, songs, and skits. Her repertoire of writings span several genres which include children's books, songs and skits; a variety of cookbooks; gardening books; short stories; and adult fiction. The core of her writings for children resonate themes of goal setting, growth, responsibility, and respect for both others and the environment. Find out more about Donna's Books by visiting her website http://www.donna-watkins.com/ and by following her on facebook and twitter. All of Donna's books are available through Amazon and Barnes & Noble

Caden Beavers provided the artwork for this book and has previously co-authored and co-illustrated a children's book (Leo the Pup who saved Christmas) with his grandmother (Donna) and illustrator Carol Dabney. Caden is very involved in his artwork as well as school and community sports such as soccer, football, trap, and archery. Caden is an outdoorsman who loves hunting and fishing.

Carol Dabney is a writer and illustrator who has provided the unique artwork for several of Donna Watkins' children's books as well as 'the cover' for this book. Carol is very talented and has written several children's books of her own which can be purchased through Amazon and Barnes & Noble.

MORE CHILDREN'S BOOKS BY DONNA WATKINS:

Nature Book Series: Hummie the Hummingbird; Hobie the Dancing Honey Bee;

The Painted Moth; For Pete's Sake; The Duck Adventures of Cheese & Quackers

Shelter Animal Book Series: Sam the Dog Pound Hound; Sophie the Shelter Cat;

Bell the Crime Fighter Dog; Leo the Pup Who Saved Christmas

Cookbooks and Gardening Books for Kids: Kidz Gone to Potz Gardening Book;

Cooking: Junior Chefs in the Game

References :

https://www.srs.fs.usda.gov/pubs/misc/ag_654/volume_2/quercus/alba.htm

https://www.fs.fed.us/database/feis/plants/tree/quealb/all.html

https://extension.psu.edu/forest-stewardship-teaching-youth-about-forest-stewardship

https://www.smithsonianmag.com/science-nature/the-whispering-trees-180968084/

https://edgeofthewoodsnursery.com/nine-reasons-plant-oak

https://www.tigtagusa.com/film/life-cycle-of-an-oak-tree-PRM00013/

https://www.thoughtco.com/how-much-of-tree-is-alive-3967213

https://en.wikipedia.org/wiki/Tree

https://www.canopyintheclouds.com/learn/canopy

https://en.wikipedia.org/wiki/Understory

https://en.wikipedia.org/wiki/Acorn

https://en.wikipedia.org/wiki/Living_stump

https://ucanr.edu/sites/oak_range//Oak_Regeneration_Restoration/Stump_Sprouting/

https://www.ncforestry.org/teachers/parts-of-a-tree/

https://www.arborday.org/trees/lifestages/

https://www.hunker.com/12486565/the-life-cycle-of-an-acorn-seedling-into-a-tree

https://homeguides.sfgate.com/many-years-can-oak-tree-produce-its-first-acorn-104502.html

https://sciencing.com/about-6325114-information-forest-ecosystem.html

https://homeguides.sfgate.com/oak-trees-bloom-66716.html

https://www.woodlandtrust.org.uk/blog/2019/06/tree-lifecycle/

http://texastreeid.tamu.edu/content/howTreesGrow/

http://txforestservice.tamu.edu/main/popup.aspx?id=209)

http://fruitandnuteducation.ucdavis.edu/generaltopics/TreeGrowthStructure/Photosynthesis_Respiration/

https://www.thoughtco.com/trees-and-the-process-of-photosynthesis-1342630

https://homeguides.sfgate.com/many-years-can-oak-tree-produce-its-first-acorn-104502.html

https://homeguides.sfgate.com/fast-white-oak-tree-grow-70719.html

https://homeguides.sfgate.com/fastest-growing-diseaseresistant-oak-trees-26449.html

https://www.thoughtco.com/common-oaks-north-america-4174951

https://sciencing.com/white-oak-trees-6521703.html

https://www.smh.com.au/lifestyle/how-trees-send-out-news-bulletins-20160825-gr0q1c.html

https://www.theatlantic.com/science/archive/2017/04/trees-have-their-own-songs/521742/

https://www.livescience.com/27802-plants-trees-talk-with-sound.html

https://www.calacademy.org/explore-science/do-plants-hear

https://dengarden.com/gardening/the-effect-of-music-on-plant-growth

http://www.bbc.com/earth/story/20141111-plants-have-a-hidden-internet

https://www.livescience.com/27802-plants-trees-talk-with-sound.html

https://www.ncbi.nlm.nih.gov/pmc/articles/PMC5797535/

https://www.treehugger.com/natural-sciences/injured-plants-warn-neighbors-danger.html

https://www.the-scientist.com/features/plant-talk-38209

https://hort.ifas.ufl.edu/woody/how-trees-grow.shtml

https://ca.audubon.org/conservation/how-plant-oak-tree-acorn

https://www.thoughtco.com/how-to-plant-an-acord-1343543

http://www.wisconsincountyforests.com/education/products-from-trees/

http://goexplorenature.com/2013/04/7-ways-kids-can-help-save-trees.html

https://www.treepeople.org/resources/tree-benefits

http://homeguides.sfgate.com/list-windpollinated-trees-44660.html

http://www.explainthatstuff.com/wood.html

Companion Song for Sprout the Mighty Oak – Sing Along

A Place To Call Home

Everyone needs a place to stay

Feel safe and cozy - store food away

A shelter from storms and raise their young

A place to stay until winter is done

_____

Elephants and Tigers live in - the Forest

Frogs and Ducks live in - the Pond

Sharks and Whales live in the Sea

Birds Squirrels and **Monkeys** - live in Trees

_____

Oh, Everyone needs a place to stay

Feel safe and cozy - store food away

A shelter from storms and raise their young

A place to stay until winter is done

_____

Lions and Bears live in - the Forest

Fish and Snakes live - in the Pond

Jellyfish and Dolphins live in the sea

Owls and **Raccoons** - live in Trees

_____

Well, Everyone needs a place to stay

Feel safe and cozy -   store food away

A shelter from storms and raise their young

A place to stay until winter is done

Wolves and Deer live in - the Forest

Beavers and Turtles live in - the Pond

Seals and Penquins live in the Sea

Skunks and **Possums** - live in Trees

Yes, Everyone needs a place to stay

Feel safe and cozy - store food away

A shelter from storms and raise their young

A place to stay until winter is done

Nature gave all – some – space- to - roam

And a place - to - call - Our - Home

Order CD "A Place To Call Home" by Donna Watkins Online at www.amazon.com

Credits: Lyrics by Donna Watkins - - - Instrumentals and Vocals by Dave McKinney

www.ingramcontent.com/pod-product-compliance
Lightning Source LLC
Chambersburg PA
CBHW080905120626
46555CB00008B/2966